![Barbie]

Wedding Party!

By Mary Man-Kong
Illustrated by Kellee Riley

A Random House PICTUREBACK® Book

Random House 🏠 New York

BARBIE and associated trademarks and trade dress are owned by, and used under license from, Mattel, Inc.
Copyright © 2013 Mattel, Inc. All Rights Reserved.
www.barbie.com
Published in the United States by Random House Children's Books, a division of Random House, Inc.,
1745 Broadway, New York, NY 10019, and in Canada by Random House of Canada Limited, Toronto.
No part of this book may be reproduced or copied in any form without permission from the copyright owner.
Pictureback, Random House, and the Random House colophon are registered trademarks of Random House, Inc.
ISBN: 978-0-307-93116-0
randomhouse.com/kids   Printed in the United States of America   10 9 8 7 6 5 4 3

Barbie and her sisters are excited—their cousin Kristen is getting married!

"I'd love it if you'd be my junior bridesmaids!" Kristen says to Barbie, Skipper, and Stacie. "And Chelsea, you will make the cutest flower girl ever!"

"We'd love to!" the sisters exclaim.

There's a lot to do, so Barbie and her sisters go with Kristen to the bridal store.

"What do you think?" Kristen asks as she tries on her wedding gown.

"Your dress is made for a princess! It's absolutely perfect on you!" Barbie gushes.

"I love that it twirls! Such a beautiful outfit for your special day!" Stacie tells Kristen.

"So cool!" says Skipper.

"And I think Chelsea and Lacey look great in my gloves and veil," Kristen says with a laugh.

Next, Barbie, Skipper, and Stacie try on their dresses.
"Too flowery!" says Barbie.

"Too many ruffles," says Skipper.

"Too puffy! I can't twirl in this,"
says Stacie.

Then they each try on one more dress.
"Too-rrific!" says Chelsea.
"Too good to be true!" all the girls exclaim.
"Those dresses are pretty on all of you!" Kristen says, beaming.

Next, Barbie helps Kristen pick out the flowers for her bouquet.

"This reminds me of when we played wedding as little girls," says Kristen.

"You used to love it when I put purple flowers in your hair. How about purple and white roses for your bouquet?" asks Barbie.

"Purple is still my favorite color!" exclaims Kristen.

Afterward, Kristen and her fiancé, Michael, invite Barbie and her sisters to help choose their wedding band.

All the bands sound great, but Kristen and Michael finally decide on their favorite.

"The Glitter Girlz totally rock!" Barbie exclaims.

The big day is finally here!
Kristen, Barbie, Skipper, Stacie, and Chelsea go to the beauty
salon bright and early to get their hair and nails done.

"I feel like a pretty, pretty princess!" says Chelsea.

At the wedding, Chelsea sprinkles flower petals as she walks down the aisle.

"You are the most beautiful bride in the whole world," Barbie whispers to Kristen before she and her sisters follow Chelsea.

At the reception hall, Barbie's cell phone suddenly rings.

"Oh, no!" cries Barbie. "The band is stuck in traffic, and the reception is about to start! Kristen is going to be so disappointed!"

"I have an idea," says Skipper. "We know all the songs—we can do it! Kristen will be so surprised!"

Skipper quickly hooks up her music player to the hall's sound system.

Barbie, Stacie, and Chelsea take the stage and sing Kristen and Michael's wedding song. The happy couple dances their first dance together as husband and wife. The crowd cheers!

"You guys are awesome!" Kristen says as she hugs Barbie, Skipper, Stacie, and Chelsea. "Thanks so much for rocking my wedding!"

"It was a lot of fun—and the best wedding party ever!" Barbie says with a smile.